SUPERBUNS!

Kindness Is Her Superpower

DIANE KREDENSOR

ALADDIN
New York   London   Toronto   Sydney   New Delhi

ALADDIN

An imprint of Simon & Schuster Children's Publishing Division

1230 Avenue of the Americas, New York, New York 10020

First Aladdin hardcover edition July 2019

For information about special discounts for bulk purchases, please contact Simon & Schuster Special Sales
at 1-866-506-1949 or business@simonandschuster.com.

The Simon & Schuster Speakers Bureau can bring authors to your live event. For more information or to book
an event contact the Simon & Schuster Speakers Bureau at 1-866-248-3049 or visit our website at www.simonspeakers.com.

Book designed by Laura Lyn DiSiena and Heather Palisi

The illustrations for this book were rendered digitally.

The text of this book was set in Mr. Stickman and Drawzing.

Manufactured in China 0419 SCP

2 4 6 8 10 9 7 5 3 1

Library of Congress Control Number 2018949084

ISBN 978-1-4814-9068-9 (hc)

ISBN 978-1-4814-9069-6 (eBook)

For Charlie Kilgras, kind *and* super

Superbuns was super kind.

listening ears

big caring
eyes

warm
happy smile

fluffy tail
(It's just cute!)

huge
heart

She loved being kind, no matter what her big sister, Blossom, said.

Blossom was 100 percent positive superheroes have powers like . . .

And as Blossom always told Buns:

Kind is kind,

Blossom was a know-it-all.
She knew *everything* about everything.

I know EVERYTHING about EVERYTHING.
Fact: kangaroos cannot hop backward. And I know that almonds are a member of the rose family! And fact: dinosaurs lay eggs! And fact: the planet Venus spins backward. Fact: bumbershoot is another word for umbrella. Two facts: an ostrich's eye is bigger than its brain, and a peanut is not a nut.
And I know you can't eat hot cobbler without cold milk. So c'mon!

The bunnies were on their way to Grammy's with a fresh-baked, piping-hot carrot cobbler.

Blossom thought all this kindness was slowing them down.

But Buns couldn't help being super.

Even to her sister.

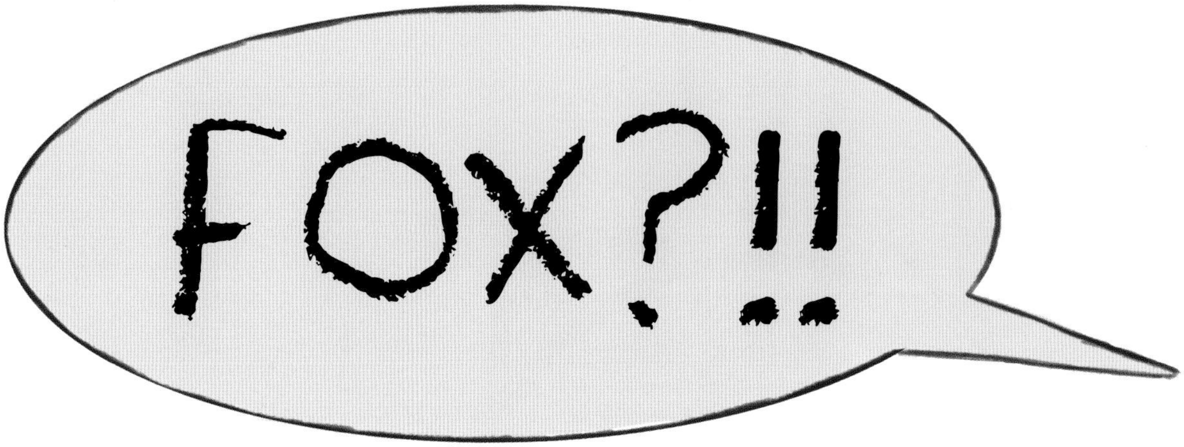
FOX?!!

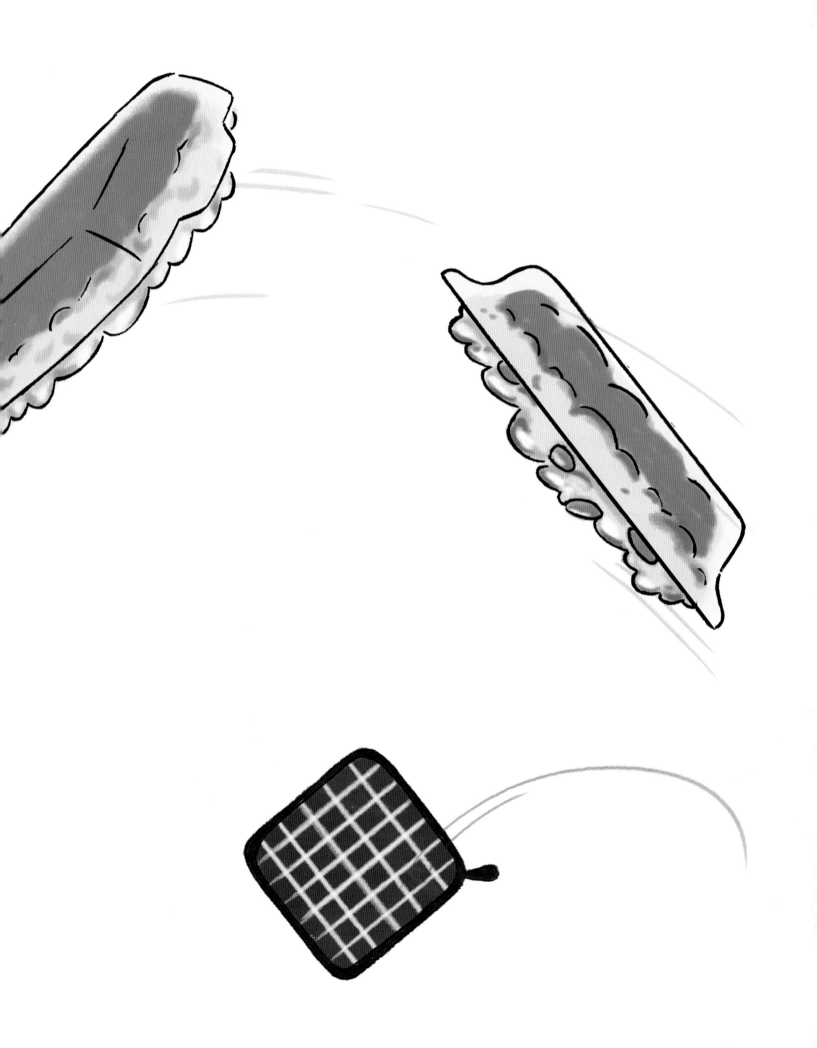

Blossom knew **exactly** what to do.

Blossom was speechless . . . almost.

I know EVERYTHING about being lost.
Did you know that the most common lost items
are keys, phones, eyeglasses, and shoes? Once, Buns lost
her homework, and I found it in Miss Lin's flowerpot. The lost city
of Atlantis has never been found. And Roanoke was the Lost Colony.
I know that the letters in "lost" can also spell "lots" and "slot"
and that "lost" is the past tense form of "lose."
And Grammy once told me that I am never
lost for words.

And just like that, Blossom learned she
didn't know *everything* about everything.

Maybe Buns was right. . . .

Maybe being kind was kind of . . . super.